THE BLUE TABLE

Chris Raschka

Greenwillow Books
An Imprint of HarperCollins*Publishers*

For Maya, Mina, Catherine, Leyla,
Kate, Dan, and Lydie

The Blue Table
Copyright © 2020 by Chris Raschka
All rights reserved. Manufactured in Italy.
For information address HarperCollins Children's Books,
a division of HarperCollins Publishers, 195 Broadway, New York,
NY 10007.
www.harpercollinschildrens.com

Watercolor and cut-paper collage were used to prepare
the full-color art.
The text type is ChaletCyr, NewYorkEighty
·
Library of Congress Cataloging-in-Publication Data is available.

ISBN 978-0-06-293776-6 (hardback)

First Edition

20 21 22 23 24 ROT 10 9 8 7 6 5 4 3 2 1

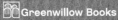 Greenwillow Books

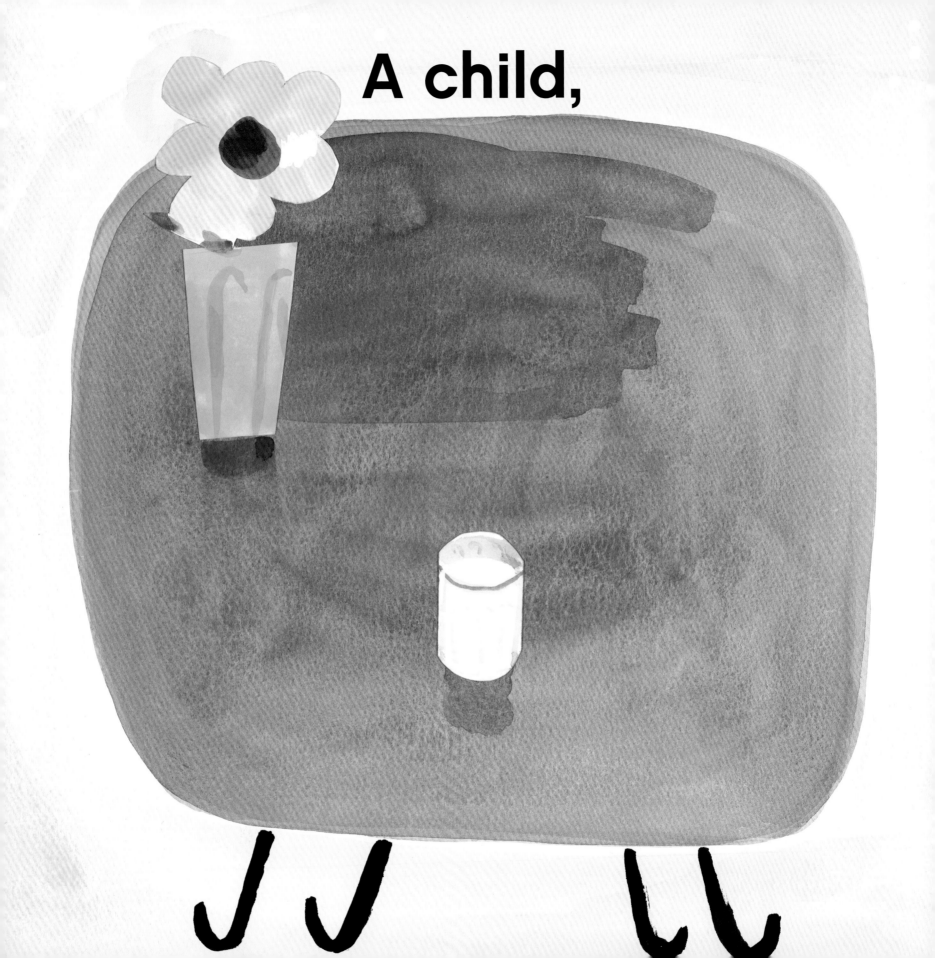

a parent,

get going.

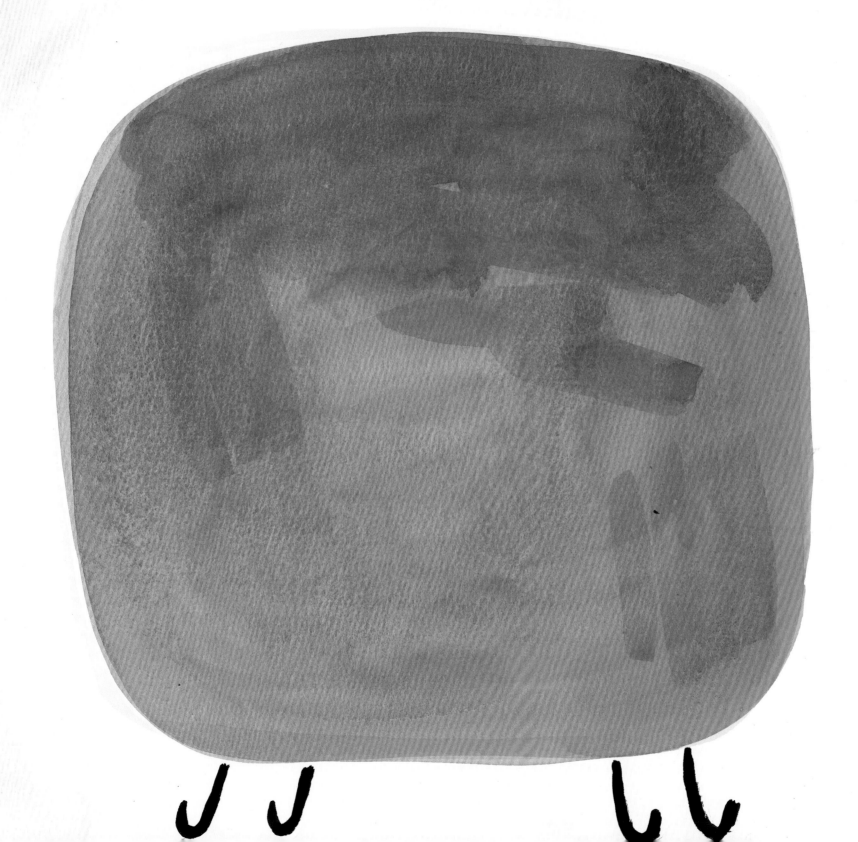

Good things

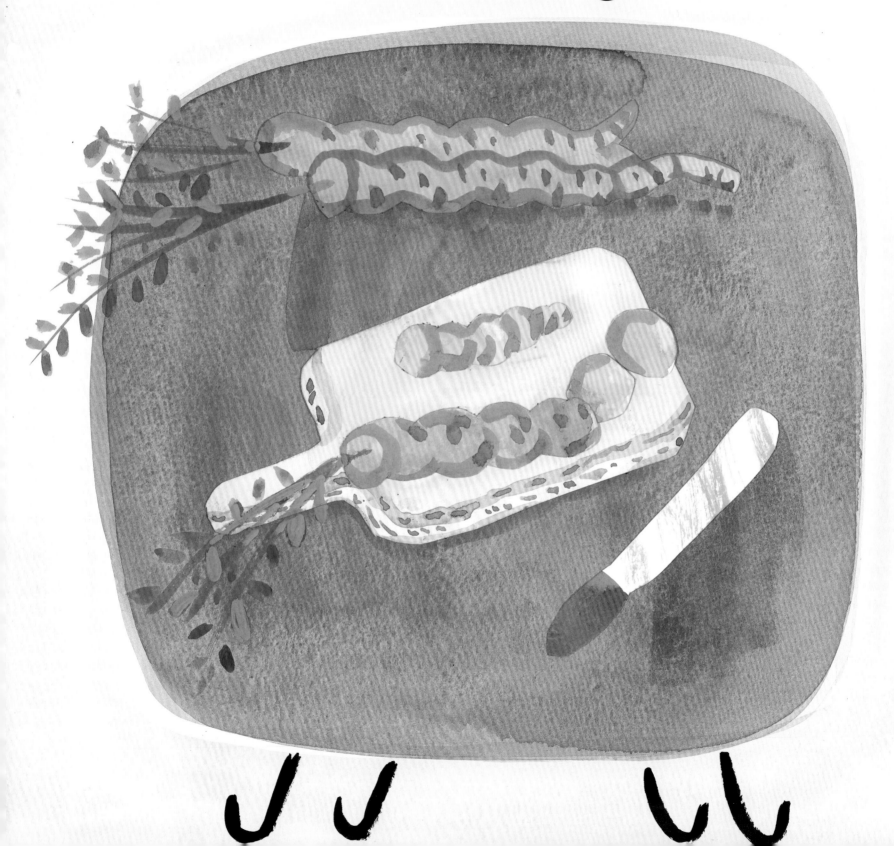

the store,

and the farm,

apples

and flowers,

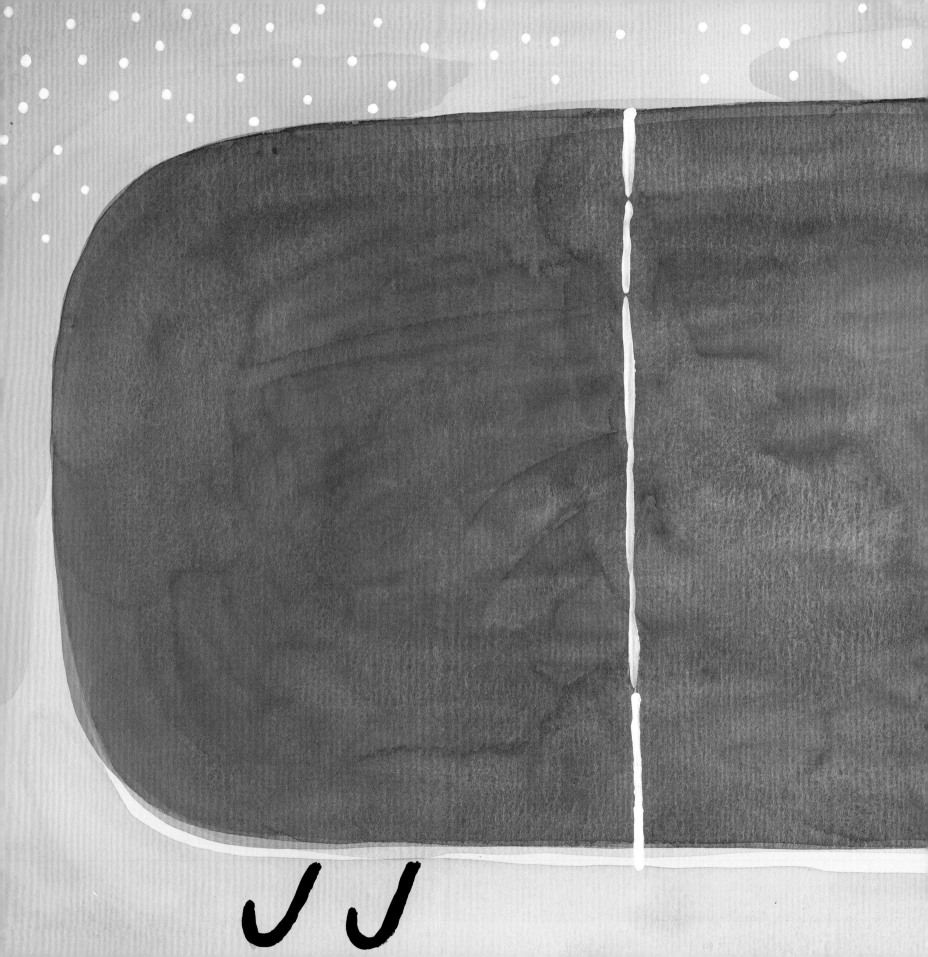

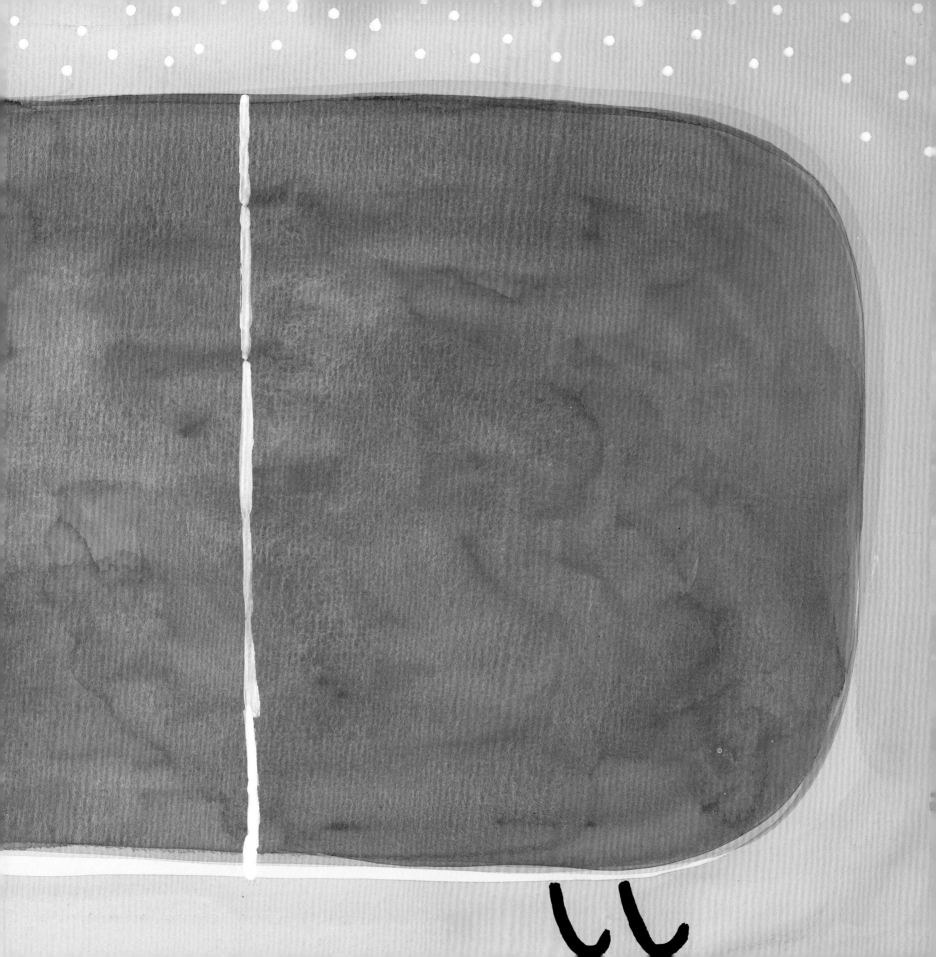

come together—

around

the
blue
table.